MOLOKA'I

MAUI

LANA'I

KAHO'OLAWE

HAWAI'I

Hilo

THE BIG ISLAND

POPOKI's
Incredible Adventure at the
VOLCANO

Written by
Diana C. Gleasner

Illustrated by
Andrea Evans Winton

Aloha Nui Loa
To
Hunter Stanton Killman
and
Heath Walker Killman

*May your dreams
come true*

Library of Congress Catalog Card Number: 99-74605
ISBN 0-9651185-5-X

Marjorie Storch Graphic Design, Charlotte, NC

Printed in Hong Kong

Popoki shivered with excitement. He and Leilani were going to fly in an airplane to visit Tutu, Leilani's grandmother, on the Big Island of Hawai'i.

When Leilani asked Tutu if she could bring Popoki, her grandmother said, "Of course. I think a real Hawaiian cat like Popoki should see the Big Island."

The trip from Kaua'i to the Big Island took two hours. Popoki did not like flying. Airline rules said a cat must travel in a cage. Popoki did not like rules.

Tutu met them at the Hilo airport. She kissed Leilani, placed a beautiful flower lei around Leilani's neck and a small crown of flowers on Popoki's head. "Popoki," said Tutu looking him over, "the Hawaiian word for cat. A fine name for a fine cat. Aloha and welcome to the Big Island." Popoki felt very important.

"Why is the air all smoky?" asked Leilani.

"Volcano fog," explained Tutu. "We call it vog. It's steam from the volcano. You remember hearing about Pele, the fire goddess who lives in the volcano. Pele cooks up a lot of vog. She's definitely in charge around here."

"Can we go to the volcano?" asked Leilani.

"Yes," promised Tutu, "but you must stay close to me and pay attention to the rules. Popoki will have to stay home. The volcano can be a very dangerous place."

Rules. Rules. Rules. Popoki was tired of hearing about rules.

"Come and see my new home," said Tutu. "Do you remember my old house down by the ocean, Leilani? Pele sent a river of red-hot lava down the mountain, and my house was in the way."

"We only had two days to get out," remembered Tutu. "We loaded everything into our truck and watched our house burn down. Then we moved to Volcano Village high up on the volcano, away from the lava flows."

"What does Pele look like?" asked Leilani.

"Some people say she's old and wrinkled with white hair," answered Tutu. "Some say she has long black hair and wears a red dress. I've never seen her, but I've seen her work. She can destroy anything in her path, and she can also create new land. Sometimes she's gentle and loving, but she has a terrible temper. She's a very powerful woman."

"Pele must be the strongest woman in the whole world,"
said Leilani.

Popoki liked Tutu's new house. He chased geckos around the yard. He jumped up on Tutu's screen door trying to catch a gecko.

"Don't hurt our geckos," scolded Tutu. "We like them. Geckos eat bugs."

Don't do this and don't do that. Popoki didn't like rules.

His feelings were hurt. He thought Tutu must like geckos better than cats. He looked around for something else to do.

Popoki tried to catch a red and black butterfly sitting on a
purple flower. The butterfly flew away. Popoki scampered after it.

The butterfly fluttered from flower to flower. Popoki chased
after it.

The butterfly flitted from yard to yard. Popoki followed.

The butterfly disappeared into the trees. And so did Popoki.

The butterfly flew over jagged black lava fields that cut
Popoki's feet. He wished he had wings like the butterfly.

The butterfly came to a high cliff and kept going. Popoki had
to stop. Huge waves crashed far below against the cliff. He
watched the butterfly until it disappeared.

Popoki was tired. He wanted to go home. He started back up the mountain. The fiery hot lava burned his paws. He came to a steaming river of molten lava.

Popoki went the other way but came to another river of lava.
He could not go any farther.

Popoki was trapped between two lava flows and the ocean. Where was Tutu's house? Where was Leilani? The air smelled smoky. It was hard to breathe, and his eyes stung. He started to whimper.

Suddenly, a tall woman in a red dress appeared. She had long black hair and bare feet. "Hello, little Popoki. What are you doing here?"

Popoki wondered how she knew his name. He let the woman pick him up. "Next time, little Popoki," she said, "listen to your Tutu."

When the barefoot woman whispered in Popoki's ear, the earth trembled.

Popoki shuddered as the woman moved slowly through the steaming river of lava. He shut his eyes tight.

The woman in the red dress carried him for miles and miles over craggy lava fields until they reached a cool green rain forest. Gently, she put him down. "Run home, Popoki," she said.

At last Popoki found Tutu's house. Everyone was happy to see him. Tutu put some lotion on his burned paws. Leilani hugged Popoki so hard he could hardly breathe.

Tutu gave him a bowl of mahimahi. Fish for dinner! It was
Popoki's favorite food.

After dinner, Popoki stretched and yawned.

He fell asleep and dreamed about a red and black butterfly
and a tall woman in a red dress.

Glossary

aloha - *ah-LOW-ha* - hello; goodbye; the spirit of love

gecko - *gek-oh* - small lizard found in the Hawaiian islands

Hawai'i - *hah-WAI-ee* or *hah-VAI-ee* - Islands in the Pacific Ocean; 50th state of U.S.A.

Kaua'i - *kau-(W)AH-ee* - one of the Hawaiian islands

lava - *la-va* - molten rock that comes out of a volcano

Leilani - *lay-LON-ee* - girl's name

mahimahi - *ma-hee-ma-hee* - Hawaiian fish

Pele - *pay-lay* - mythological fire goddess who lives in the volcano

popoki - *po-po-kee* - Hawaiian word for cat

Tutu - *too-too* - Hawaiian word for grandmother

vog - *vog* - volcano fog, steam from erupting volcano

volcano - *vol-cane-oh* - vent in earth's crust that spews out lava and steam from time to time

Author - Diana C. Gleasner

Diana had a longtime dream of one day living in Hawaii. She, her husband Bill, and their two children, Suzanne and Stephen, moved from Buffalo, New York, to the Hawaiian island of Kauai.

While the family was camping on Kauai's Na Pali coast, 12-year-old Suzanne Gleasner adopted a starving kitten. She named it Popoki. The kitten survived many adventures and became a much loved member of the family.

A writer for more than thirty years, Diana Gleasner has written thirty books as well as countless magazine and newspaper articles. She received a B.A. from Ohio Wesleyan University and M.A. from the State University of New York at Buffalo. The Gleasners now live in North Carolina.

Illustrator - Andrea Evans Winton

Andrea has been a graphic artist and illustrator for more than twenty-five years. Her fine arts work has won many awards and is part of collections throughout the United States and Great Britain.

Illustrating children's books has been Andrea's lifelong dream. Her formal art education was at Brook's Institute of Fine Arts in Santa Barbara, California. Currently Andrea acts as the Gallery Coordinator at the Mariposa County Arts Council's "Fifth Street Gallery" in Mariposa, California, just outside Yosemite National Park. She is continuing her freelance art career in her spare time.

Thanks to Irene Haughey of Cat Furr Productions (Mariposa) and her "Fabulous Felines" for providing purrfect inspiration.

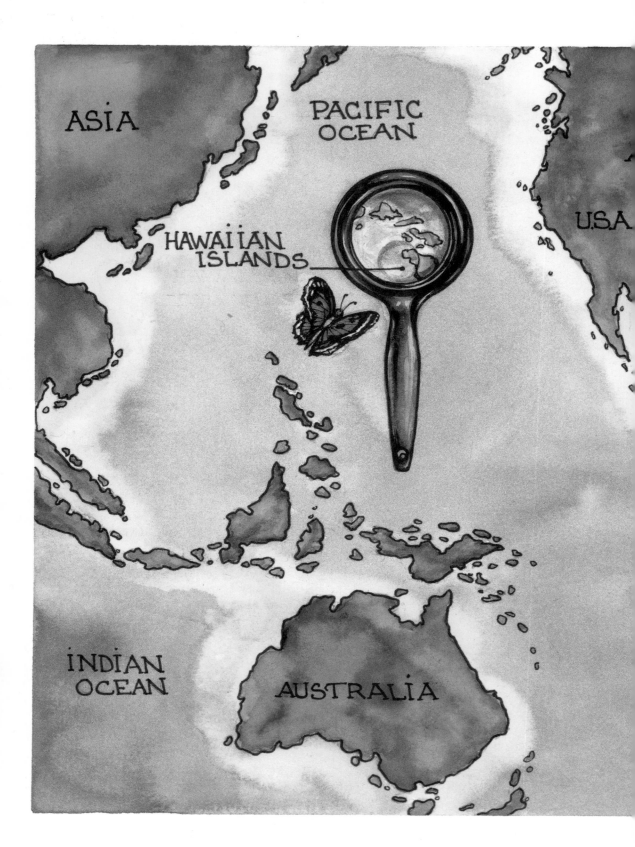